WELCOME... THE 3D ACTIVI...

GW00402330

Pedigree

Published 2011. Published by Pedigree Books Limited
Beech Hill House, Walnut Gardens, Exeter, Devon, EX4 4DH
email: books@pedigreegroup.co.uk
web: www.pedigreebooks.com

[Contents]

£6.99

REY MYSTERIO

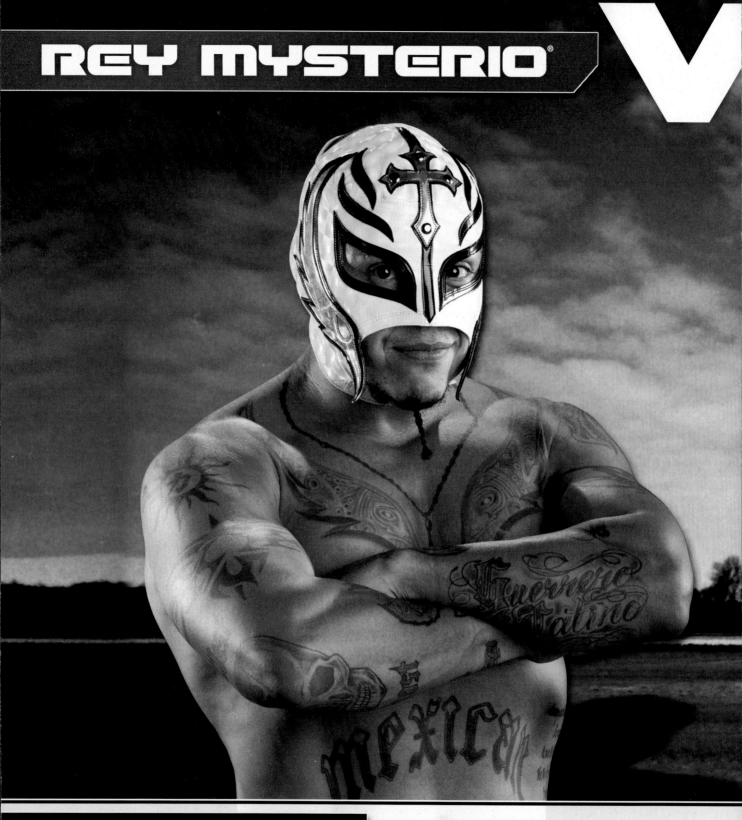

The meanest rivalry heading into *SummerSlam 2010* centred on champion Kane and Rey Mysterio over the cherished World Heavyweight Championship.

Leading up to their big showdown, Kane's brother, Undertaker, defeated Mysterio to qualify for the Fatal 4-Way Match for the World Heavyweight Championship at Fatal 4-Way. However, Undertaker, was later found in a 'vegetative state' by Kane, leaving the self-professed Devil's Favorite Demon on a mission to find out just who had caused the near-fatal damage.

All roads led him to Mysterio, who turned the

accusation on its head, claiming that Kane had in fact attacked his own brother. There would be only one way to settle the dispute once and for all – in the squared circle of course – and Kane looked to have gained his revenge once and for all. With a chokeslam, backed up with a Tombstone, Mysterio was literally at death's door. But just as Kane tried to put the masked one in an adjacent casket there was a massive surprise in store.

Undertaker had returned to cast his judgment, but on which side would he fall? Brotherly love or the Ultimate Underdog? Turn over to follow the action…

"Ouch! A Mysterio blow to the face leaves The Big Red Monster red with rage!"

"Rey won't be taken out of the squared circle easily, but he finds Kane's right boot too hot to handle!"

"Hey look, it's role reversal time – now Rey's keeping Kane outside the ring!"

"Time for some more air time as Rey flies into Kane!"

"But he's the Heavyweight champ for a reason and proves too strong yet again!"

"Kane is right on top of his game with this backbreaker. Painful, painful, PAINFUL!"

"But Mysterio somehow pulls himself back from the brink and we know what's coming…"

" but has he seen Kane's fist coming in the other direction?"

"And it's curtains for Mysterio as a tombstone leaves him heading for the casket!"

"A victorious Kane says this is revenge for his brother Undertaker!"

"But look at that! Look at that! Out of the casket comes Undertaker himself!"

"He wants some answers NOW. Just who did leave him in a vegetative state?"

"Looking into the eyes of Mysterio, he's now convinced it wasn't him!"

"And instead unleashes his anger out on the Devil's Favorite Demon!"

"They may be brothers but Kane won't take this as he prepares for another chokeslam!"

"And finishes off with the second Tombstone of the night! Is there no end to this man's power!"

13

QUIZ PART ONE:

There's no better feeling in the world than to lift a treasured championship belt high in the sky. There are six titles up for grabs in the world of WWE but how much do you know about them all?

WWE Championship

1 "I defeated Sheamus in a Six Pack Elimination Challenge at Night of Champions in September 2010 to win the WWE Championship. My middle name is Keith and my father is a 'Cowboy'."

2 "I picked up my first WWE Championship in December 2009 when I defeated John Cena – but then lost out to him just three months later in an Elimination Chamber Match."

United States Championship

1 "This is my first reign as the United States Champion. I defeated The Miz in September 2010 at Night of Champions in Illinois."

2 "I also beat up The Miz to take the vacant title in May 2010. It was my first championship since I returned to WWE. What's Up!"

World Heavyweight Championship

1 "I am the oldest champion, having debuted in WWE in 1997. I won the title at Money in the Bank match in July 2010. I defeated Rey Mysterio."

2 "I was the inaugural World Heavyweight Champion when I was awarded the title in September 2002 by Eric Bischoff. You might also know me as Hunter Hearst Helmsley."

THE ROAD TO GLORY

Use the stickers in the book to match the WWE champions to the clues given below.

Intercontinental Championship

1 "I defeated Kofi Kingston on SmackDown in August 2010. I then retained the title at SummerSlam."

2 "In December 2009 I managed to pin John Morrison after he mocked my Scottish roots, at Tables, Ladders and Chairs – it was my first championship in WWE."

WWE Tag Team Championship

1 "Alongside my partner Drew McIntyre we defeated The Hart Dynasty in a Tag Team Turmoil Match at Night of Champions in September 2010."

2 "I picked up the championship title with my buddy Big Show in February 2010 following a Triple Threat Elimination Match that also involved the Straight Edge Society."

Unified Divas Championship

1 "I defeated Melina in a Title Unification Lumberjill Match at Night of Champions. You'll know me as part of Team Lay-Cool."

2 "I am the longest-reigning champion, having held the title from December 2008 to July 2009. You may know me as Ted DiBiase's personal assistant."

WORDSEARCH

Can you find the ten WWE Superstars hiding in this wordsearch? You'll have to take a close look because they are more difficult than a Rey Mysterio finishing move!

Santino Marella	☐	Cody Rhodes	☐
Chris Jericho	☐	The Miz	☐
Finlay	☐	CM Punk	☐
Hornswoggle	☐	MVP	☐
Layla	☐	Mark Henry	☐

S	S	C	H	R	I	S	J	E	R	I	C	H	O	P	R
L	A	Y	A	L	K	N	U	P	M	T	C	O	D	Y	R
G	M	N	A	L	W	F	I	N	L	A	Y	R	M	F	Y
S	F	C	T	V	O	U	Y	E	S	D	A	N	A	I	M
S	C	L	M	I	C	M	M	C	P	U	N	S	R	N	A
E	O	H	A	I	N	S	U	A	Z	L	R	W	K	L	R
D	D	O	T	Y	Z	O	P	L	I	J	Y	O	Y	A	L
O	Y	R	T	R	L	U	M	Y	M	R	T	G	R	E	K
H	R	N	H	E	I	L	C	A	L	F	H	G	N	M	R
R	H	S	Z	H	A	P	A	L	R	B	E	L	E	V	A
Y	O	W	I	T	P	U	L	Y	Z	E	M	E	H	G	H
D	S	C	M	P	U	N	K	E	L	B	L	D	K	C	H
O	R	M	E	I	I	M	O	H	G	L	T	L	R	M	E
C	H	I	H	S	R	T	Z	X	M	V	P	A	A	P	N
L	C	Z	T	G	A	P	T	F	C	W	S	D	M	U	R

CROSSWORD

Using all your WWE knowledge, can you work out the clues below to fill in this teasing yet tasty crossword?

The Down Clues
1. Irish star who pinned John Cena to win his second WWE Championship
2. A legend who retired in 2010 after losing to Undertaker
3. Formed The Legacy with Cody Rhodes and Randy Orton
4. Evan - a tag team partner of Mark Henry

The Across Clues
5. Money in the Bank Ladder Match winner at *WrestleMania XXVI*
6. Three times the eighth letter in the alphabet!
7. Known for his Attitude Adjustment
8. His masks make him a mystery man
9. Intercontinental Champion after defeating Kofi Kingston

17

DOLPH ZIGGLER

Dolph Ziggler put his Intercontinental Championship on the line against Kofi Kingston at SummerSlam 2010 but The Nexus ensured it was a no contest.

KOFI KINGSTON™

The Nexus' brutal assault left Kingston battered and bruised, but he lived to fight another day against Ziggler.

ALL MIXED UP

Can you guess these Superstars of WWE by rearranging the mixed up letters? Use the stickers to put their names in the correct places. We've also added a clue underneath in case you are extra stuck!

ROYTRANDON

Clue:

His signature move is the RKO

BARYLANEIDN

Clue:

Former NXT rookie trained by Shawn Michaels

LIACIFXOA

Clue:

Diva Champion in the summer of 2010

DIKYTOSND

Clue:

Signature move is the Sharpshooter

MOJHORNSORIN

Clue:
Known as the Monday Night Delight on RAW

TURKENDEAR

Clue:
Ended Shawn Michaels' career in the ring

YELLKLYELK

Clue:
Joined a trio of Divas called Extreme Exposé

KENMAHRRY

Clue:
The World's Strongest Man!

WHO'S THAT?

LOOK AT THESE SIX PICTURES OF CURRENT WWE SUPERSTARS

CAN YOU IDENTIFY WHO THEY ARE, BY JUST A SECTION OF THE IMAGE?

1

2

3

1. ? ? ? ? ? ?

2. ? ? ? ? ? ?

3. ? ? ? ? ? ?

4. ? ? ? ? ? ?

5. ? ? ? ? ? ?

6. ? ? ? ? ? ?

RANDY ORTON

The biggest rivalry from *Raw* heading into *SummerSlam 2010* was between the champion Sheamus and Randy Orton over the WWE Championship.

In the build up, The Viper let out all his venom to defeat Edge and Chris Jericho in a Triple Threat match, earning the right to face the Celtic Warrior – but he knew that a defeat would be a disaster. Defeat would mean he would not battle for the championship again while Sheamus was top dog.

Using his sizeable weight advantage, the pasty one used his brute force to grab the upper hand early in the match, only for the fangs

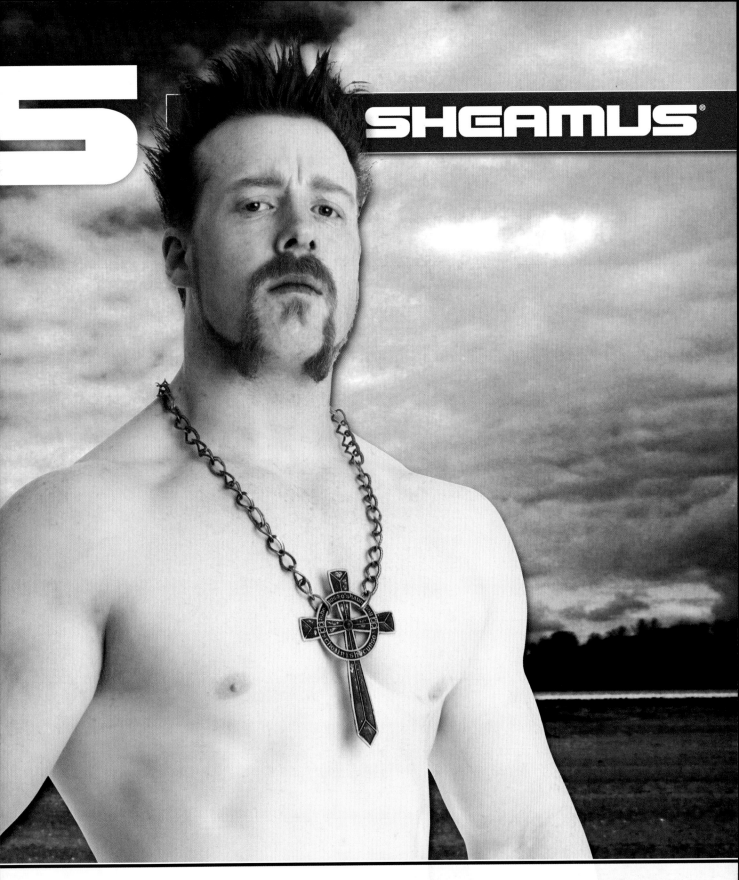

to come out of Orton – and it was soon clear whose side the crowd was on inside a packed STAPLES Center in Los Angeles.

The pair traded blow after blow: Sheamus unleashing a clothesline, while Orton reversed a suplex, much to the crowd's approval. This was too close to call but after the challenger kicked out of a Brogue Kick,

an enraged Sheamus went looking for his customary help outside the ring. A steel chair came into his sight lines only for the referee to interfere. A struggle ensued, resulting in a disqualification for Sheamus.

But if you thought that was it, think again... these two just don't know when to call it a day! Now turn over to follow the action...

"Here's Sheamus showing off his WWE Championship belt loud and proud!"

"But Randy's in the zone. He's ready for business!"

"The champ shows off his credentials with a mean looking headlock!"

"But it doesn't take long for The Viper to get his fangs into Sheamus!"

"The Celtic Warrior is angry and counters with a move of his own!"

"Orton's deadly kick leaves Sheamus as pale as the canvas. Ouch!"

"Randy repeats the feat. Just how can Sheamus come back from that!"

"Orton now goes for the DDT to add insult to injury!"

"Sheamus clings to the rope. He's gonna be eating the floor any time soon!"

"But the ropes belong to Sheamus and it's Orton who's now heading for the exit door!"

"You can't keep a good man down. The Viper snaps back. He wants it outside the ring!"

"Sheamus is only too happy to oblige!"

"Back inside the ring Orton kicks out but his opponent is wise to the game!"

"That's what we've been waiting for! Randy Orton hits the RKO!"

"Now Sheamus lashes out but it's a pain game all around!"

"Orton's in an armlock. The title looking safe with the Warrior!"

"Outside again and Sheamus is heading for the barricade!"

"There's time for one more dose of pain...."

"...but Orton kicks out of a Brogue Kick. Sheamus is enraged!"

"He goes looking for a steel chair. That means just one thing - disqualification!"

"Randy now can't win the title. He's angry and goes for an RKO on the announcers' table!"

"Sheamus is left in a state of shock. He wasn't ready for this!"

"The headphones are ready but Sheamus is in no condition for an interview!"

"It's frustration for Orton but at least he can milk the applause with a moral victory!"

QUIZ PART TWO:
SMACKDOWN vs RAW

They are world famous brands known the world over but how much do you know about *RAW* and *SmackDown?* Take our 10 question test on both to see if you are a brand expert.

RAW Question 1

The opening theme to *Raw* is 'Burn It To The _ _ _ _'

██████████

by Nickelback

RAW Question 2

In August 30, 2010, *Monday Night Raw* reached a landmark episode. Was it the 800th, 900th or 1000th episode?

RAW Question 3

General Manager Bret Hart fired the season one winner of *NXT* after he had earlier helped storm the *RAW* set. But what is his name?

RAW Question 4

RAW _ _ _ _ _ _

was a special show that featured Chad Ochocinco last year.

RAW Question 5

Can you name this *Raw* star who hails from Moscow?

32

RAW VS SMACKDOWN

Use the outlines as a clue and find the sticker that helps answer each question...

SMACKDOWN Question 1

The opening theme to *SmackDown* is 'Let It _ _ _ _'

by Divide The Day

SMACKDOWN Question 2

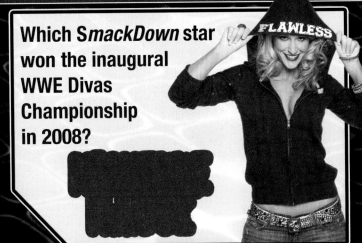

Which *SmackDown* star won the inaugural WWE Divas Championship in 2008?

SMACKDOWN Question 3

In what year did *SmackDown* launch – 1995, 1997 or 1999?

SMACKDOWN Question 4

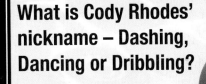

What is Cody Rhodes' nickname – Dashing, Dancing or Dribbling?

SMACKDOWN Question 5

Kofi Kingston comes from Africa but do you know which country?

This is Gail Kim vs Michelle McCool at *Bragging Rights* earlier this year. Can you spot the ten differences between these pictures of the stunning duo in action on the night?

MATCH'EM UP

Take a look inside the WWE locker room. It's an exclusive place where the Superstars of the WWE Universe get a chance to gather their thoughts and prepare for the rumble ahead – but can you identify which locker belongs to which Superstar?

| The Great Khali® | John Cena® | MVP® | Drew McIntyre™ | Luke Gallows™ | John Morrison™ |

TEAM WWE

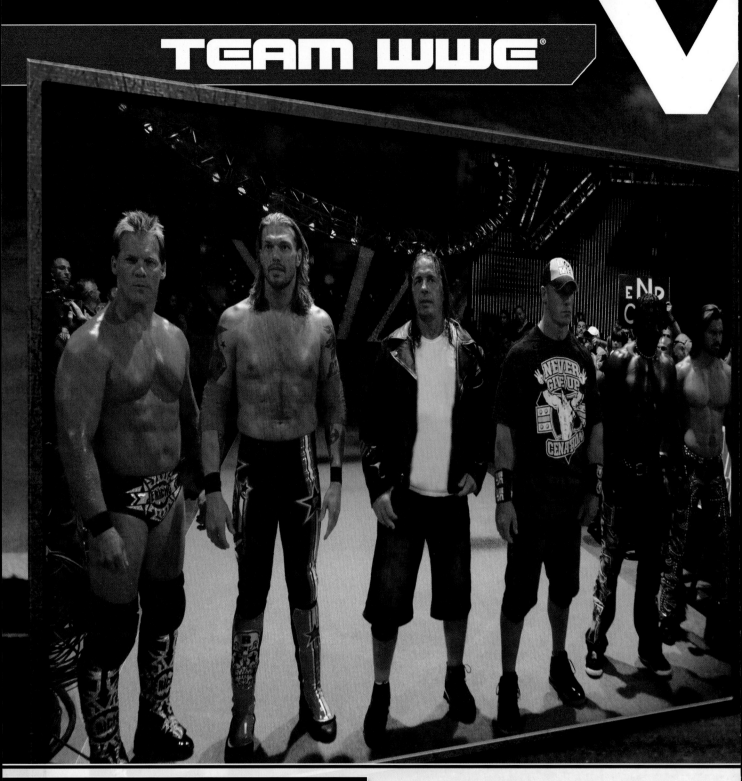

Talk about getting ideas above their station, The Nexus – a stable consisting of former WWE NXT rookies led by Wade Barrett – had already made their debut before *SummerSlam 2010*, causing mayhem and mischief to John Cena, CM Punk and a number of the ringside crew as they got more and more desperate in their attempt to guaranteed WWE contracts.

The decision was left to then-General Manager Bret Hart, who steadfastly refused, and was himself attacked as a result.

And so began a number of discriminate yet frequent attacks on WWE Superstars, crew and legends – although Cena bore the brunt, costing him his cherished WWE Championship on two occasions.

This outrageous behaviour could continue no

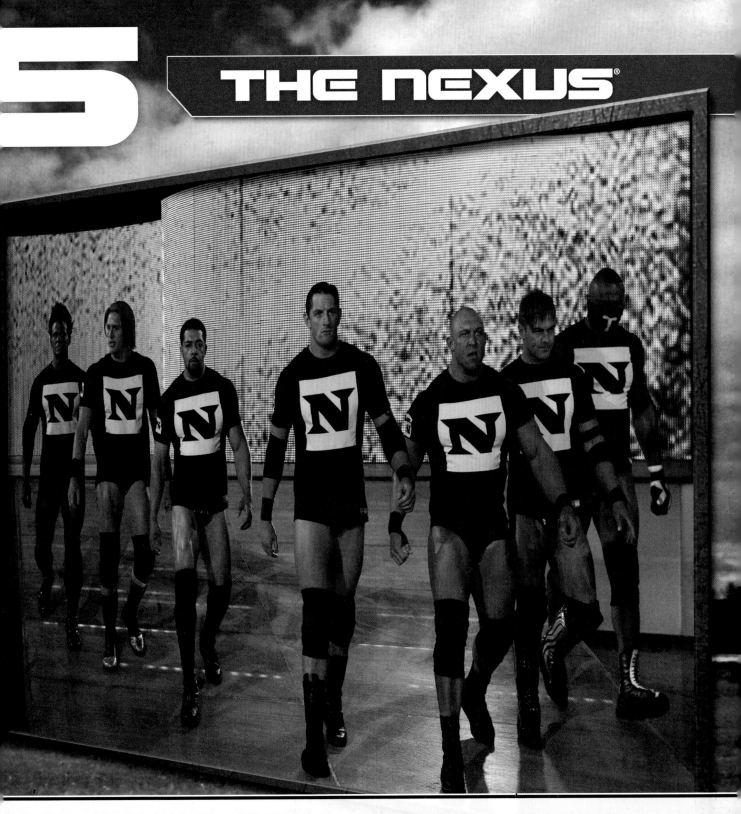

longer and there would be just one way of settling the ongoing carnage – inside the ring at *SummerSlam!*

So step forward Edge, Chris Jericho, John Morrison, R-Truth, Bret Hart and Cena himself - Team WWE – for a match-up that captured the imagination of wrestlers and fans alike.

Just one thing, with this being a 7-on-7 Elimination Tag Team Match, the math didn't quite add up. Team WWE might have been the hot favourites, as was proved on the night, but they remained a man down.

So who would be their lucky seventh member? Step forward Daniel Bryan to help exact the best revenge ever on those upstarts with attitude. Now turn the page and follow the action…

"The Nexus boys look mean and moody. This, they hope, is their time to shine!"

"But if they want the respect of the WWE Universe, they've got to beat John Cena and Team WWE first!"

"And you've got to be brave or plain crazy to take on these superstars!"

"Daniel Bryan made his intentions clear. He can't wait to take on Darren Young!"

"He locks Young in a crossface submission and Young taps out!"

"It's not going the way of The Nexus. Time for a rethink!"

"R-Truth is tagged next and nails Justin Gabriel with his fast hands. Ouch!"

"And he hands out twice the pain with a thunderous suplex. Double ouch!"

"John Morrison also shows of his air skill to take out Michael Tarver!"

"There's double trouble as Tarver and Gabriel take R-Truth out!"

"Next in is Chris Jericho but he's met his match as Wade Barrett gets him into a submission hold!"

"It's time for Skip Sheffield to try and match the might of Morrison!"

"Bret Hart comes in and nails Heath Slater straight away!"

"With such awesome power, it's little wonder Slater has become friends with the canvas!"

"It's not Gabriel's night as Edge spears him into the ropes. Feel his pain!"

"But the roles are reversed as Edge clings on for dear life!"

"He's right on the Edge now as Barrett gets into the Rated-R Superstar!"

"The Walls of Jerico come crashing down on David Otunga!"

"So who's gonna enter the ring next? John Cena and Edge fight for the right!"

"Cena is down, but it's Edge and Chris Jericho who are eliminated!"

"Daniel Bryan lends John Cena some much-needed encouragement!"

"It's paid off as Cena fights back and lashes out at Justin Gabriel!"

"And it's all 'kicking off' as Daniel Bryan takes out Heath Slater with some fancy footwork!"

"Bryan's looking mean and moody. Who's next?"

"The Miz, that's who! The Money in the Bank briefcase is heading for Bryan's head!"

"Wade Barrett attacks John Cena – as the last man standing this looks terminal for Team WWE!"

"But look at that! Gabriel goes for the 450 splash but misses!"

"Cena hits back with the five-knuckle shuffle and Gabriel is out!"

"The Nexus cannot believe what is happening. They looked home and dry!"

"You just can't keep a good man down and Cena does the STF to win the day!"

"Who's the man? Cena's the man!"

"Cena is the lone survivor and Team WWE are the victors!"

"???
IN PEACE"

⑥

⑧ "I'M A
RATED R
????????"

①"YOU CAN'T
??? ME"

"IT'S GONNA B
JUST LIKE ME
ABSOLUTELY
?????????"

SAY
WHAT!

50

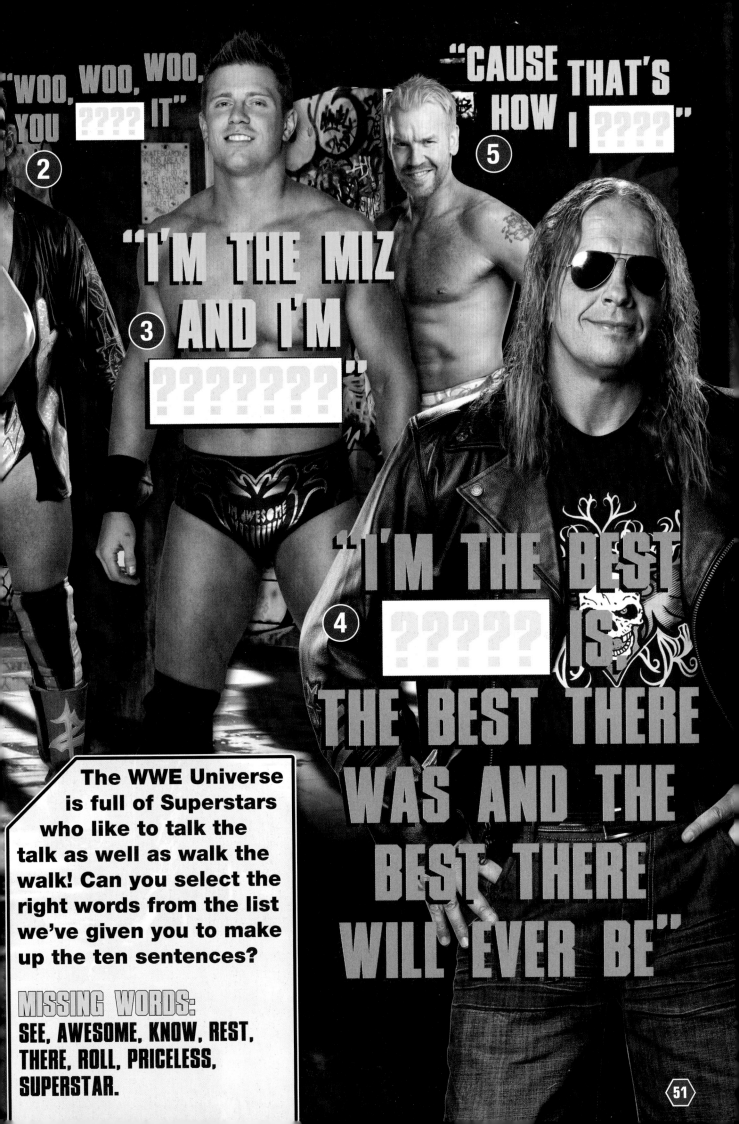

"WOO, WOO, WOO, YOU ????? IT"

2

"I'M THE MIZ AND I'M ???????"

3

"CAUSE THAT'S HOW I ????"

5

"I'M THE BEST ????? IS THE BEST THERE WAS AND THE BEST THERE WILL EVER BE"

4

The WWE Universe is full of Superstars who like to talk the talk as well as walk the walk! Can you select the right words from the list we've given you to make up the ten sentences?

MISSING WORDS:
SEE, AWESOME, KNOW, REST, THERE, ROLL, PRICELESS, SUPERSTAR.

BIG SHOW®

The World's Largest Athlete showed all his might to put the Straight Edge Society firmly in the shade at *SummerSlam 2010.*

CM PUNK®

The foundations of the SES were rocked to the core after CM Punk was put to the sword by Big Show at *SummerSlam 2010*.

W QUIZ PART THREE:

The WWE Universe is full of Superstars of all personalities, shapes and sizes. Some have been around the block for years, others are new to the squared circle, but how much do you know about the older generation and new kids on the block?

Old Skool Question 1

Where does the Undertaker come from?

A. Death Valley

B. Death Street

C. Death Town

Old Skool Question 2

Edge lost a World Heavyweight Championship to who in 2010?

A. John Cena

B. Big Show

C. Chris Jericho

Old Skool Question 3

What was the name of the movie John Cena starred in?

A. The Marine

B. The Pilot

C. The Warrior

Old Skool Question 4

Who is Kane's brother?

A. Undertaker

B. Big Show

C. Jack Swagger

Old Skool Question 5

In which country did Rey Mysterio start his wrestling career?

A. Spain

B. Argentina

C. Mexico

OLD SKOOL VS NEW COOL

New Cool Question 1

What is the name of Jimmy Uso's brother?

A. John

B. Jey

C. Josh

New Cool Question 2

Who was Kaval's mentors in the second season of NXT?

A. Team LayCool

B. Straight Edge Society

C. The Uso Brothers

New Cool Question 3

Who did David Otunga submit to in SummerSlam 2010?

A. John Cena

B. R-Truth

C. Chris Jericho

New Cool Question 4

Daniel Bryan beat who to win the WWE United States Championship in 2010?

A. The Miz

B. Cody Rhodes

C. Dolph Ziggler

New Cool Question 5

What country does Wade Barrett come from?

A. England

B. Scotland

C. Northern Ireland

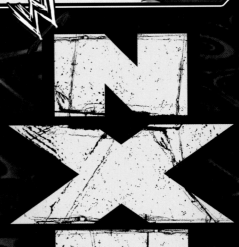

STRAIGHT EDGE
SCRAMBLE

LUKE GALLOWS

SERENA

CM PUNK

JOEY MERCURY

CM Punk, Luke Gallows, Serena and Joey Mercury are in a rush for their big showdown with Big Show. Only one of them will get to the ring on time but who will it be?

BIG SHOW

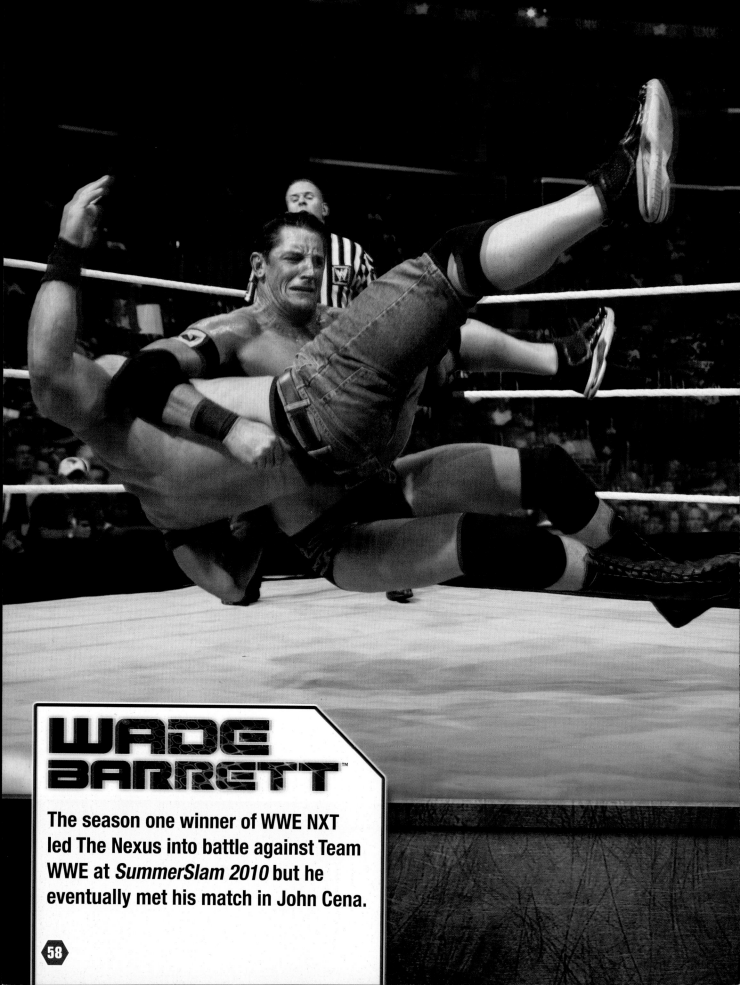

WADE BARRETT™

The season one winner of WWE NXT led The Nexus into battle against Team WWE at *SummerSlam 2010* but he eventually met his match in John Cena.

DAVID OTUNGA™

The fourth member of The Nexus to bite the dust in the seven-on-seven Tag Team match, Otunga fell under The Walls of Jericho.

LIGHT AND HEAVY

Name: Big Show®
Height: 7-foot
Weight: ??? Pounds
From: Tampa, FL
Move: Chokeslam, Cobra Clutch, Backbreaker

Name: Undertaker®
Height: 6-foot-10.5
Weight: ??? Pounds
From: Death Valley
Move: Chokeslam, Tombstone, Last Ride

Name: Rey Mysterio®
Height: 5-foot-6
Weight: ??? Pounds
From: San Diego, CA
Move: 619; West Coast Pop

We've got six of the biggest stars from the WWE Universe on the scales to see how much they weigh.

Reckon you can match them up correctly?

Name: The Great Khali®
Height: 7-foot-3
Weight: ??? Pounds
From: India

Name: John Cena®
Height: 6-foot-1
Weight: ??? Pounds
From: West Newbury, MA
Move: Attitude Adjustment, STF

Name: Hornswoggle™
Height: 4-foot-4
Weight: ??? Pounds
From: Dublin, Ireland
Move: Tadpole Splash

420

129

485

240

175

299

JOHN CENA®

When it comes to a rumble against Team Nexus, who better to lead Team WWE at *SummerSlam 2010* than John Cena? The upstarts were put in their place and Cena certainly played his part!

UNDERTAKER®

While The Undertaker made an unexpected entrance at *SummerSlam 2010*, he was handing out a shock of his own against Kane.

WORDSEARCH

Can you find eight NXT stars from the first two seasons hiding in this wordsearch? Take a close look as they're harder to spot than Undertaker in his casket!

Justin Gabriel	☐	Alex Riley	☐
Daniel Bryan	☐	David Otunga	☐
Percy Watson	☐	Kaval	☐
Wade Barrett	☐	Michael Tarver	☐

J	D	S	I	R	R	A	H	Y	K	S	U	H	D	H
U	A	R	M	P	Y	E	L	I	R	X	E	L	A	U
S	N	T	I	I	A	L	E	X	R	I	L	E	V	S
T	I	R	C	R	C	M	S	R	I	L	E	F	I	K
I	E	N	H	C	E	T	A	E	O	V	A	N	D	H
N	L	O	A	Y	T	T	K	S	Y	N	S	O	O	A
G	B	S	E	H	H	E	A	C	H	K	X	P	T	R
A	R	T	L	U	A	R	C	O	P	Y	A	E	U	K
B	Y	A	T	N	V	R	L	N	S	E	A	V	N	A
R	A	W	A	K	A	A	A	K	K	H	R	T	G	V
I	N	Y	R	Y	L	B	U	G	L	A	T	C	A	A
E	N	C	V	H	A	E	D	U	L	A	V	A	Y	P
L	A	R	E	A	V	D	V	B	E	E	V	A	E	E
F	D	E	R	R	A	A	A	D	U	J	G	A	B	H
A	A	P	E	R	C	W	D	J	U	S	T	I	K	R

CROSSWORD

Using all your NXT knowledge, can you work out the clues below to fill in this tough tackling crossword?

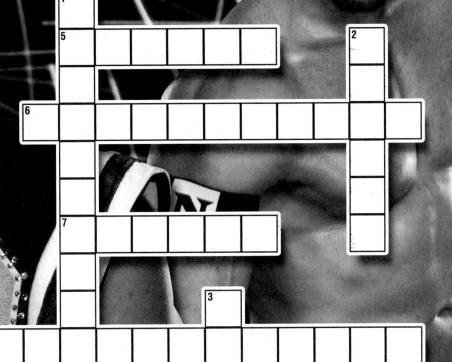

The Down Clues
1. Winner of season one
2. Daniel Bryan's pro in season one
3. Season two winner
4. This Team was 3 Down's pros

The Across Clues
5. The Diva wannabe is being guided by Goldust
6. Christian was the mentor to this season one contestant
7. David Otunga asked this guy 'Wassup?'
8. This Superstar has an angel for a surname
9. The Miz mentored this guy in season two

QUIZ PART FOUR:

WWE Superstars come from all corners of the globe, but can you match them up with their rightful homes...

Drew McIntyre:
"Och aye, we play the bagpipes!". I am from...

? ? ? ? ? ? ?

Sheamus:
"They call my homeland the Emerald Isle". I am from...

? ? ? ? ? ?

PLACE NAMES:

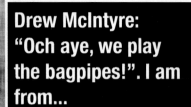

ENGLAND, INDIA GHANA, SCOTLAND, IRELAND, RUSSIA, JAPAN & ITALY

William Regal:
"We love fish and chips and The Queen where I'm from!". I am from...

? ? ? ? ? ?

1. William Regal   2. Vladimir Kozlov   3. Kofi Kingston   4. Sheamus

WHERE IN THE WORLD?

Santino Marella: "Mama Mia! We love pizzas and a leaning tower!". I am from...

? ? ? ? ?

Vladimir Kozlov: "There is a Red Square where I live and it's cold in the winter!". I am from...

? ? ? ? ? ?

Kofi Kingston: "I'm from Africa but do you know where?" I am from...

? ? ? ? ?

The Great Khali: "I like to visit the Taj Mahal when I go home". I am from...

? ? ? ? ?

Yoshi Tatsu: "I'm from the land of the Rising Sun". I am from...

? ? ? ?

5. Yoshi Tatsu   6. Drew McIntyre   7. Santino Marella   8. The Great Khali

ANSWERS...

P14-15. WWE Quiz Part One.
1. Randy Orton, 2. Sheamus; 3. Daniel Bryan, 4. R Truth; 5. Kane, 6. Triple H; 7. Dolph Ziggler, 8. Drew McIntyre; 9. Cody Rhodes, 10. The Miz; 11. Michelle McCool, 12. Maryse.

P16. Wordsearch.

S	S	C	H	R	I	S	J	E	R	I	C	H	O	P	R
L	A	Y	A	L	K	N	U	P	M	T	C	O	D	Y	R
G	M	N	A	L	W	F	I	N	L	A	Y	R	M	F	Y
S	F	C	T	V	O	U	Y	E	S	D	A	N	A	I	M
S	C	L	M	I	C	M	M	C	P	U	N	S	R	N	A
E	O	H	A	I	N	S	U	A	Z	L	R	W	K	L	R
D	D	O	T	Y	Z	O	P	L	I	J	Y	O	Y	A	L
O	Y	R	T	R	L	U	M	Y	M	R	T	G	R	E	K
H	R	N	H	E	I	L	C	A	L	F	H	G	N	M	R
R	H	S	Z	H	A	P	A	L	R	B	E	L	E	V	A
Y	O	W	I	T	P	U	L	Y	Z	E	M	E	H	G	H
D	S	C	M	P	U	N	K	E	L	B	L	D	K	C	H
O	R	M	E	I	I	M	O	H	G	L	T	L	R	M	E
C	H	I	H	S	R	T	Z	X	M	V	P	A	A	P	N
L	C	Z	T	G	A	P	T	F	C	W	S	D	M	U	R

P17. Crossword.

[Crossword grid answers: SHEAMUS, JACKSWAGGER, SHOWNMICHAEL, TRIPLEH, JOHNCENA, REYMYSTERIO, EDDIEBASE, ZIGGLER, BOURNE]

P20-21. All mixed up.
1. Randy Orton, 2. Daniel Bryan, 3. Alicia Fox, 4.Tyson Kidd, 5. John Morrison, 6. Undertaker, 7. Kelly Kelly, 8. Mark Henry.

P22-23. Who's that?
1. Edge, 2. John Morrison, 3. Mr McMahon, 4. Undertaker, 5. Alicia Fox, 6. The Great Khali.

P32-33. WWE Quiz Part Two.
Raw: 1. Ground, 2. 900th, 3. Wade Barrett, 4. Roulette, 5. Vladimir Kozlov.
SmackDown: 1. Roll, 2. Michelle McCool, 3. 1999, 4. Dashing: 5. Ghana.

P34-35. Spot the Difference.

P38-39. Match Em Up.
1. MVP, 2. Luke Gallows, 3. Drew McIntyre, 4. John Cena, 5. John Morrison, 6. The Great Khali.

P50-51. Say What.
1. See, 2. Know, 3. Awesome, 4. There, 5. Roll, 6. Rest, 7. Priceless, 8. Superstar.

P54-55. WWE Quiz Part Three.
Old Skool: 1.A, 2.C, 3.A, 4.A, 5.C. New Cool: 6.B, 7.A, 8.C, 9.A, 10.A.

P56-57. Straight Edge Scramble.
CM Punk gets to the ring to face Big Show.

P60-61. Heavy and Light.
Big Show 485 pounds, The Great Khali 420 pounds, John Cena 240 pounds, Rey Mysterio 175 pounds, Undertaker 299 pounds, Hornswoggle 129 pounds.

P64. NXT Wordsearch.

J	D	S	I	R	R	A	H	Y	K	S	U	H	D	H
U	A	R	M	P	Y	E	L	I	R	X	E	L	A	U
S	N	T	I	I	A	L	E	X	R	I	L	E	V	S
T	I	R	C	R	C	M	S	R	I	L	E	F	I	K
I	E	N	H	C	E	T	A	E	O	V	A	N	D	H
N	L	O	A	Y	T	T	K	S	Y	N	S	O	O	A
G	B	S	E	H	H	E	A	C	H	K	X	P	T	R
A	R	T	L	U	A	R	C	O	P	Y	A	E	U	K
B	Y	A	T	N	V	R	L	N	S	E	A	V	N	A
R	A	W	A	K	A	A	A	K	K	H	R	T	G	V
I	N	Y	R	Y	L	B	U	G	L	A	T	C	A	A
E	N	C	V	H	A	E	D	U	L	A	V	A	Y	P
L	A	R	E	A	V	D	V	B	E	E	V	A	E	E
F	D	E	R	R	A	A	A	D	U	J	G	A	B	H
A	A	P	E	R	C	W	D	J	U	S	T	I	K	R

P65. NXT Crossword.

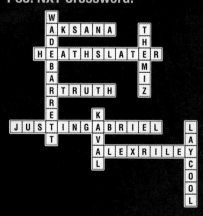

[Crossword grid answers: WADEBARRETT, AKSANA, HEATHSLATER, THEMIZ, RTRUTH, JUSTINGABRIEL, KAVAL, ALEXRILEY, LAYCOOL]

P66-67. WWE Quiz Part Two - Where in the World.
1. England, 2. Russia, 3. Ghana, 4. Ireland, 5. Japan, 6. Scotland, 7. Italy, 8. India.

GROUND ROLL ROULETTE

MICHELLE McCOOL VLADIMIR KOZLOV GHANA 1999